American

By Alfred Brock

American. By Alfred Brock.

This book is a collection of images and poems of American Indians – Americans.

The Human Experience is not bounded by shapes. It is not fenced in by color. It is not limited to one language. It is not one set of laws.

The Human Experience is not exclusionary.

January 4, 2023

INTRODUCTION

War is no good.

'Whether you are right or wrong, whether you win or lose, in no circumstances can war help you or your country.'

– Arthur Ponsonby

I live in Michigan now.

Many Native American tribes live here. I would like to learn more of the languages. Especially the words for the places that are here and were here.

The images in this book are of Ojibwe, Apache, Cherokee and some others.

These were black and white images that have been treated with a computerized system. Life is not black and white.

"Let us put our minds together and see what life we can make for our children."

-Sitting Bull

Joy in laughter

Sunny day

Some face brightened

Humor spilling

Out like sunshine

Sound of Summer grass

Spring Rain

Autumn Leaves

Winter crackling

No time for worry

No time

In laughter

Spill out

Cover the land

Building

Making

Fashioning

The canoe

Light

Ancient built frame

Finished

Carried by two men

Carries two tons

Note made

Confirmation

Understanding from one man

How

Is it

Communication stops

Trail of Tears

Named

Trail

Carrying weary

Families

Carried away

Soldiers

Warriors

Cooking by fire

Waiting

Traversing

Resettlement

From Forest Kingdom

To Grass Plain

Where are the buffalo?

Where the homes?

Where is my family?

Cold weather

Miles upon

Miles upon

A nation rises up

Settled

Towns, Villages

A city

Conquerors come

Sickness comes

Settled land declared an empty wilderness

What law is that?

The hat

The hat speaks words

The mouth refrains

Across

Miles upon

Miles upon

The hat

Same from Siberia

What then

The Wilderness

With baby resting

Raising up

Playing at knees

Wading in streams

Waiting

Waking

Filled with song

Sounds of birds

Yet seen

The land is formed

Seeded

Wandering

Fort, village, town, city

Baby resting

Growing

Language of the past

Language of the future

Language spoken now

Land discovered

Knowledge

Set aside

Words strange

Language strange

The sickness

Wars

Persisting

Left in wilderness

Abandoned

Settlers and Indians

Collide

Knowing the way

Requires attention

Attention to detail

Detail of the mind

Mindful of interior

Connections to exterior

Bridging

Points

Structures and fabric

Woven

Knitted

Framed

Spun

Not Separate

Gathering the Wild Rice

Gathering the Rice

Rice

In the Winter Land

Growing

In the Winter Land

The People

Are Nourished

What is that you are eating?

The Earth

The Earth Rice

Earth Mother Food

Words foreign

Rice is life

Rice

In the Winter Land

Knowledge

Just below the surface

I will cook it

I will make it

I will combine it

I will grow it

I will save it

I will smoke it

I will preserve it

I will hang it

I will clean it

I will put it in a basket

I will wash it

I will carve it

I will cut it

I will smash it

I will squash it

I will fry it

I will bake it

I will cook it

I will eat it

Here the time comes

Like a wave

Here the time comes

Live a river swelling

Can you see it?

Can you hear it?

Can you taste it?

Can you smell it?

Can you feel it?

Here the time comes

For growing

For harvesting

For preparation

For cooking

For eating

For cooperation

Here the time comes

Standing with hunger

The New Arrivals

Bags emptying

Stomachs hungering

Eyes look out

Upon the great lakes

Laid out before them

The empty lands

Filled with people

Suffering

The hunger

Man, woman and child

What is your need?

Hungering for food

The People show the People

The land is rich

It cannot be seen but by those

Who look

Look

It is my home

I sing my home

It is my wife

I sing my wife

It is my husband

I sing my husband

It is my life

I sing my life

Warm in Winter

Cool in Summer

It is my time

I sing my time

It is Morning

I sing Morning

It is Day

I sing Day

It is Night

I sing Night

The Family

Is Many Parts

Grandmother, Mother, Daughter

The life is known

The life is mysterious

She remembers the old ways

The way it was before

The changes that have come

Stepping back

Why do these things happen?

Sorrow comes to all

So Joy begins again

The child rearing up

Bridging woman

From time past to future place

Living in one world

Exclaiming

The forest

Like a background

When one cannot see the edges

Of each point

It is plants

Where does one sit?

There

Where does one lie down?

There

Can't you see?

It's all trees

Ha, ha

Comes the voice

Meadows, glades, streams, rivers, ponds, lakes

New Trees

Old Trees

The Forest

You in the foreground

In the Season

Cook the food

In the morning

Cook the food

In the evening

Cook the food

Songs and stories

Cook the food

Work the land

Cook the food

The Village

Is woven into the forest

Where is one part?

Where is two parts?

Cook the food today

Eat the food in winter

It is an old pot

We had them before

You came

All People are Equal

Princesses and Princes

Walk the Land

The Words Cannot Stop the Steps

The Boots Come

The Boots Stay

Princess looking out

Upon the City

Watching her people

Waiting for the day

The Passing

Much to remember

Much to recall

The Passing

They receive not

Taking

They gather empty baskets

What Language?

The Princess waits

Symbols

Government

Language

Hunting

Gathering

Farming

Fairness

Laws

Reason

Science

Religion

After the carrying

Everyone settles down

Time to eat

Time to talk

Now the Learning will Begin

It's been a long Walk

Late time

Over time

The War passed

Through time

It is over now

It is changed now

A Different War

A Different Peace

Fashioned from the ashes

Of the Roaring Times

The Time of the Beasts

We build quietly now

See how the strong rise up

The scourge is passed

Some fine dust remains

The People

It's a fine day

Is it not?

For my People

I ask this

Some food for them

I ask this

Some home for them

I ask this

No more war

I ask this

Some medicine

I ask this

Where is the water here?

Where are the animals?

Where is the forest?

I will make it

I will raise it

For my People

I ask this

Some land for them

I can tell a story

I can sing a song

I can tell a story

About what went wrong

All decided before

Like facing a hurricane

Watching it build

What softness is there

In a hard world

Making way

The Woman's Way

The Man's Way

The Child's Way

May way

You cannot see inside

If you will not

Each face a mirror

Each life is known

No secret here alone

It’s a time

For fruit

For vegetable

For meat

For water

For wisdom

Waiting for trade

What is fair trade

One side giving

One side taking

The other

Waiting for trade

Waiting

Laughter is like song

Filling the day

Building memories

Echoing into the future

Laughter is lilting music

Drifting on the wind

Bounding over hard places

How can they be happy?

Ha ha ha

How can they be not?

The sun is shining

The earth warm

Beneath their feet

Friends close by

Laughter like a river

Through time

We lift out boats

On the current

Song

The Knowledge

Waits

Beauty cannot be hidden

Long

Wisdom is not dangerous

Calm

Fear not memory

Clear

Your hands are not tied

Bound

Your actions not predetermined

Wind

The Restoration has begun

Water

All these things

I will make for you

All these things

I will make with you

I will hand you the wood

I will give you the tools

I will bring you the water

I will tend your fire

I will provide you with food

I will put the words within your mouth

I will fill your belly

I will light your mind

I will free your soul

It is all good

Thought it will be hard

It is good to be alive.

If you are going to build a house
First you must build a fire
If you are going to build a fire
First you must have a forest
If you are going to have a forest
First you must have land
If you are going to have land
First you must have a world
If you are going to have a world
First you must have a Universe
If you are going to have a Universe
First you must have a Creator

That is why we thank the Creator for fire
You
Though
Still don't know how to make it

You can walk

Where you cannot see

It seemed silly

To me

She said it again

You can walk

Where you cannot see

The Man laughed

'See? They are fools.'

He turned and walked away.

She said again

You can walk

Where you cannot see

I looked down

There, just below the surface

Were rocks

From rock to rock I passed

And so

Walked where I could not see

On the water

In Spring

To get the flour and medicine

We flow down

With furs

All at once

All the trappers are there

The price goes down

Down, down, down

Finally, no bargaining

Take it or leave it

No money flows

Direct trade

Barter is done in the morning

In the aftermath, Exchange

Furs for food

Furs for medicine

If you have not

You get not

I can see with my eyes

I can hear with my ears

I can feel with my skin

I can smell with my nose

I can taste with my tongue

It is the world around us

Me

I

You

They

Us

Altogether

What is different?

We will make the Canoe in the chilly wind

We will make the Canoe to float on the waters

It is not the way it used to be

We will all work together to make the Canoe

When it is done it will float upon the water

We will trade

I will carry the furs down the river

I will go across the lakes to trap

All these things I will do

In the old days we didn't go so far

These days they want the furs

All the time

There will be none left if they call for them more

They do not listen

If I do not go, Others will go

We need the work and money and food

It is all different today from the old stories

What will the new story be?

I cannot tell you who you are

You are who you are going to be

I cannot tell you what to do

You will do what you are going to do

I cannot tell you what to think

You will think thoughts from yourself

It is about family

About the land

About community

When I was a child

I was a child

When I was across the land

I was over there

There are many things to see and do

What will those things be for you?

That Doctor laughs, How can that work?

Old superstition!, Never can work

How did that ever work?

The child is sick

The Doctor is laughing

I have brought the medicine

Prepared it, Provided it

It took my life to learn it, to be a Doctor

Now waiting

That Doctor is checking

Checking for fever with a thermometer

As if he has no hands

'Luckily I am here', he says

Where was he

Last winter?

When the sickness came?

Some left, some stayed, that Doctor was not here

This Doctor will be here when that Doctor leaves

Days of Rain

No work

Days of Sun

Sometimes

If it’s not wet

Patching the Canoes come in from work

Gumming the new ones

Set to go out

Always with the gum

Gather the gum

Cook the gum

Prepare the gum

It must be just right

Don’t waste it

Apply it

Like this

See?

Teaching

The Canoes won’t float long without it

Creating the Canoe
Building the Canoe
Manufacturing the Canoe
Sailing the Canoe
Repairing the Canoe
Old time into the new years
Canoes across lakes
Canoes along rivers
Canoes to the harbors
Down to the ports
Towns and Villages
Furs go
Grains come
Trade it is
Trade it was
Trade it always will be

In the sunlight

The burning heat

The heat

In the soul

Through the heart

Warming the body

Skin

Like fire

Sun touching arm

We move across the desert

To the water

In the chasm

We move from the sunlight

To the sunlight

Waiting in warm darkness

For burning light of day

Across the lake

To the Trading Post

We go to the Trading Post

See?

Here the land is marked on paper

A sign there

There

No one knows

The Old Village was there

The canoes came up the river

Down the river

To the lake

To the Village

Across from the Trading Post

I take the children in

We will get some flour and soap and things

There are no streets at the Trading Post

A dock

A porch

We are working

Myself and the boy

It is a long day

But it's worth it

The Sun shines

The snow melts

Spring comes again

I call this thing a pail

I call that thing a house

Battle has a name

Conquest has a name

What is the name for the actions after the war

In many places without war

The same

The story is loud

The song, long

It becomes a waiting game

After all

What are you waiting for?

I will show you the wind
I will show you the way
It is up to you
To see it
I cannot give you my thoughts
You must think them as well
When the great cities were here
There were many of the people
Then the sickness came
Still the people were there
Then the wars came
Still the people were there
Across the great waters
Came the others
Still the people were there
But it changed
The movements
The horses
The Wars

It will be in the morning
When we walk across the land
We will go to the far place
Beginning the journey with one step
They've come to help us they say
Where were they when the sickness came?
Who was fighting the wars?
Their faces are gone.
Our faces are gone
We are still here and on they come
We cross the river and hills
It is a far land and wide
It is flatter than where we came from
The children remember the mountains
But do not see them
Nor have walked in them
We grow the corn and raise the cattle

The horses are good

They called them Factories

Factories

To make things

To collect things

Bringing things in

From the far horizon

Papers, paperwork

They brought the Telegraph

It froze

The lines broken

In gentle wind

They brought the planes

The break in Winter

When the Sun is low on the horizon

They don't fly

They brought radio

The Aurora made it crackle and sleep

Satellites now

Satellites and now they can hear

It is ancient
It is yesterday
It is today
It is tomorrow
It is modern
The words remain
Repeated
In the old times it was different living
In the new times it is difficult
How can the destroyers
Rebuild what they destroyed
We have pieces and wholes
They are clearly displayed
Where are the houses
Where are the trails
Where is the talking?
How can the Learners
Be the Teachers
Before Knowing?

Creating the day

Finding the food

Making the food

Preserving the food

Making the family

Building the home

There are all days

So many days

The snow comes

The Spring comes

It is Summer again

The Autumn sings

Winter

Look how they live, Not knowing

Before the sickness came

Towns

Before the soldiers came

Villages

Find the thing

For the medicine

Is as important

As knowing what to do

With what

For what

When

It sounds like magic

Gather then the plant

When the first Wolf Moon appears

Mouths scoff

Throats chortle

The plant grows then and is suitable for medicine

At the end of January

I have no time

To correct and I will not disdain

If you will not understand

We will go then

Out on the water

Across the water

To the other side of the lake

We will go then

Up the hill

Through the meadows

To the other side of the mountain

We will go then

Axes in hand, Hew the lumber

Take down the trees

Clear the branches

Drag the logs then

To the stream

To the river

Pulling them down then

Floating them down then

To the lake

Building the canoe

Bark, Branch, Log

Tree, bushes

Weaving rope, string, cable

Cross beams, Patching, Gumming

Everyone has a job

Tough, resilient

Gathering from far

When the traders came

It was time to go further

When the loggers came

It was time to go further

Bringing back to go out

Smaller, smaller

Fewer, fewer

When the farms came

It was time to further

Then the towns came

There was no further

Walking in the Berry Patch

It is over to the windward, to the West

Where the wind comes often

They grow low, filled full with fruitful bounty

I go

The others gathering

From late morning

Collecting

Mother, Grandmother, Sister, Wife, Brother

Grandfather, Father, Son, Daughter

Bears come later

Cubs gamboling

Rolling around and around

I watch the bears

Black mother bear

Brown father bear

The cubs

One red, One golden

Gathering in the Berry Patch

It is hard road

It is a soft road

Dust is hard

My shoes are made

With leather, cloth and parts

Waiting for the world to see

Put them on

Walk upon the hard road

Walk upon the soft road

Under the stars, Under the Sun

Dust rising, Dust rises when the rains come

Rain falls down

Puffs of dust in answer

Earth sings to herself, Drumming in water

The sound of many footsteps

Walking across the world

On a hard road

On a soft road

My shoes upon them

My Horse

Land

Walking

Walking my horse on the land

Under the sky walking my horse on the land

Trailing, seeing and noting

The Sun is high in the sky

So we will break

Wait

Then walking my horse on the land

Across the rocks and open grades

Flattened by time

Boulders rear up, growing from the ground

Cactus and Agave

Turning trail weaves

Until vista revealed

Faint trail

Dismount

Then walking my horse on the land

www.ingramcontent.com/pod-product-compliance
Lightning Source LLC
LaVergne TN
LVHW052009160826
845678LV00005B/1690

* 9 7 9 8 3 7 3 9 9 6 3 2 7 *